For Moi, my little sister!
(After all, Penelope was her mouse!)

AUTHOR'S NOTE

Penelope, The Tea Mouse is based on a true story, during the 1960s, while my little sister, Moi, and I were growing up. God Bless Mom & Dad, who actually had to put up with this mouse in the first place. Still to this day, Penelope pops up unexpectedly in our lives. Just a few weeks ago, late one night while I was trying to sleep, I heard something rattling around by my old bureau. I got up and cast my flashlight beam over in the corner of the room... and there I found Penelope...AGAIN!

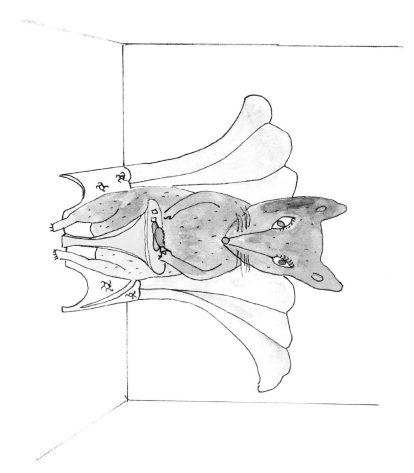

Penelope

The Tea Mouse

Written & Illustrated by Helen W. Holden

ISBN 978-0-9887269-1-8 (Hardback)

Library of Congress Number 1951451210

First Hardback Edition, February 2017

10 9 8 7 6 5 4 3 2 1

Special thanks to Katherine Gladsky for her excellent proofreading services.

Published by Holden's Whimsicals, 822 College Ave, Unit 686, Kentfield, CA 94914-0686

www.holdenswhimsicals.com

Graphic Design by Laura Almada

Printed and bound in the USA

Penelope just appeared one night on our doorstep in San Francisco. She was a medium-size brown mouse, with an oval face, large button-blue eyes, and she had a set of black whiskers on both sides of her long nose.

Penelope didn't live in a cage. Instead, my little sister fixed up a guppy tank into a little mouse-size apartment. On cold nights, to warm Penelope's space, Moi turned the tank light on.

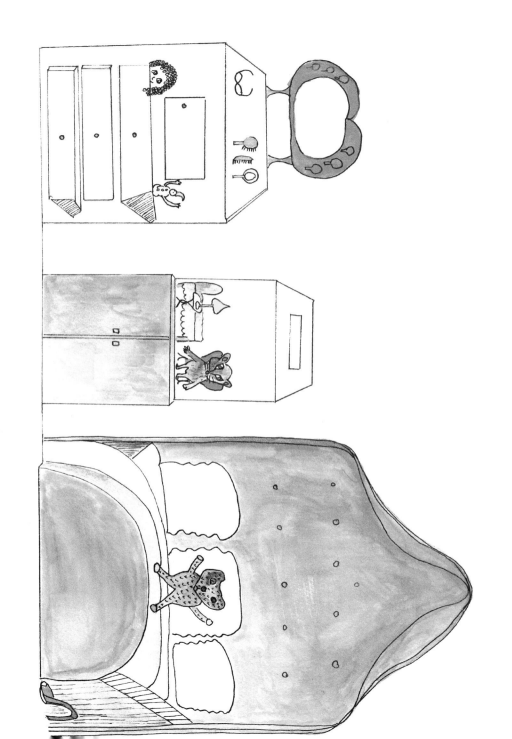

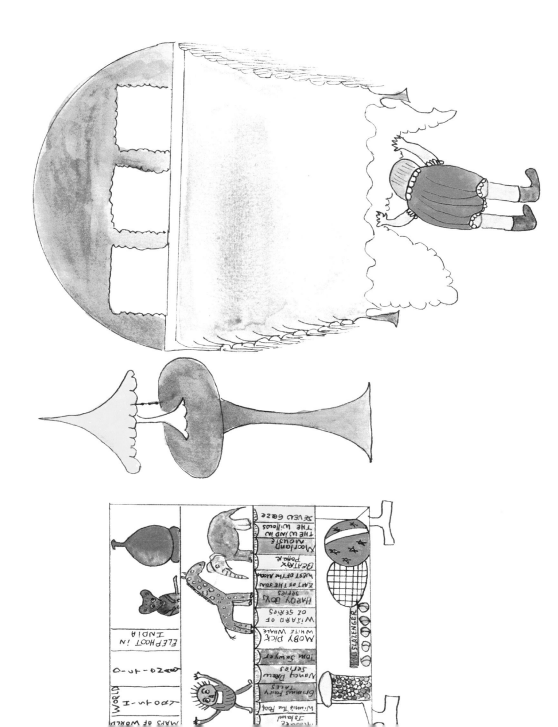

One day Penelope wasn't in her tank house. So our entire household turned the place upside down looking for Penelope.

It was Mom who found Penelope in the hall linen closet.

After that successful excursion, Penelope never stayed put in her converted tank house.

Penelope copied what we did, of course in her own way. She was fascinated with our toys. One thing I knew for certain was that Penelope was possessive and if she thought something was hers, then hers alone it became.

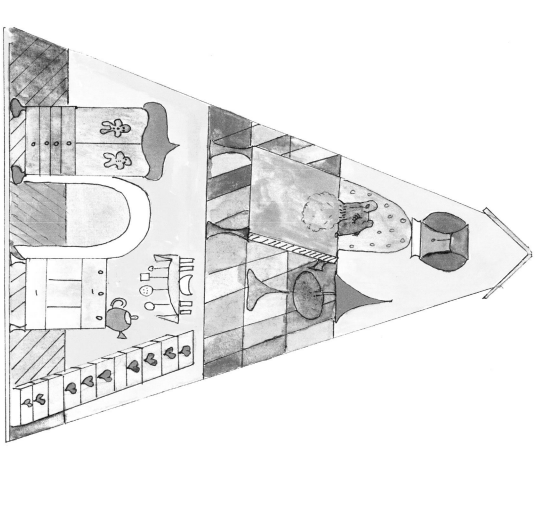

She loved my doll house! She rattled around in there and sometimes she would be as quiet as a mouse, all curled up in the attic bed. I think that she felt most at home in quarters that were her size.

Penelope usually had a great sense of balance as she explored all the rooms in our house.

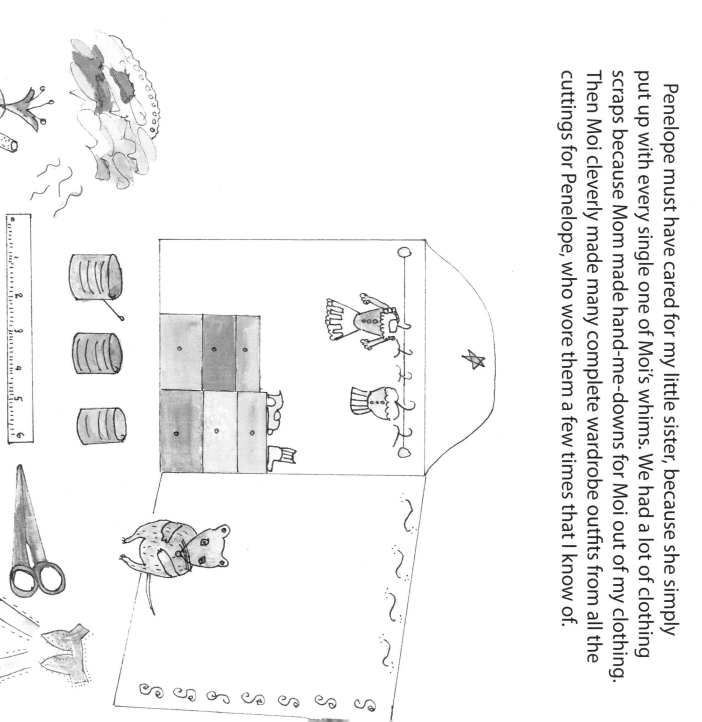

Penelope must have cared for my little sister, because she simply put up with every single one of Moi's whims. We had a lot of clothing scraps because Mom made hand-me-downs for Moi out of my clothing. Then Moi cleverly made many complete wardrobe outfits from all the cuttings for Penelope, who wore them a few times that I know of.

They say mice have a great sense of smell. Penelope discovered the shortbreads that had been procured on one of Mom and Dad's shopping trips to London. Who could imagine that this little mouse could open a fastened and secured tin?

When Penelope had time, in between her explorations, we had tea parties with friends. But mostly it was just Moi and me and Penelope.

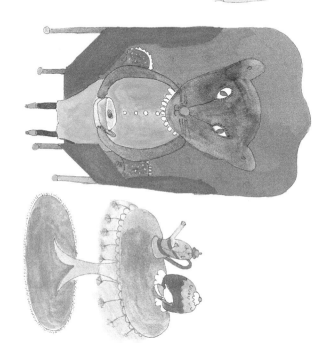

Another time Penelope disappeared and turned up when Mom found the warm and wiggly mouse inside one of her favorite high-heel shoes.

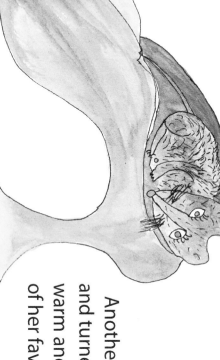

Sometimes Penelope just liked sitting and looking out the living room window.

Four years later when Moi turned twelve, we learned we were going on a trip to London with Mom and our grandmother. I felt a bit guilty talking about our trip in front of Penelope, so my sister and I would whisper about it. The day came, our suitcases were packed, and soon enough we were airborne.

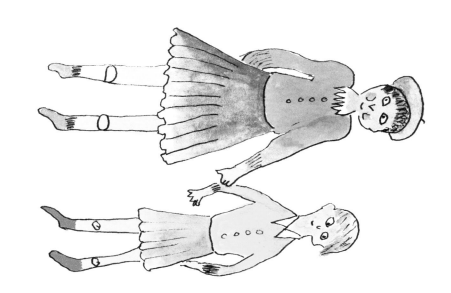

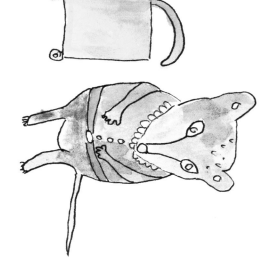

London was busy and bustling! "Bobbies" were blowing their whistles. Just as we were getting closer to our hotel, the Queen went by in her coach. The coachman was driving her team of horses from behind the carriage!

We had quite forgotten about Penelope!

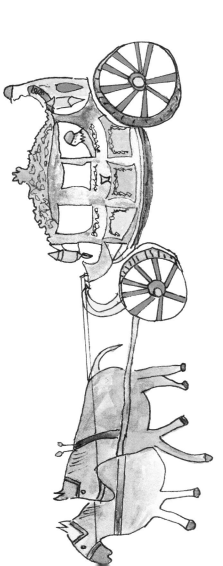

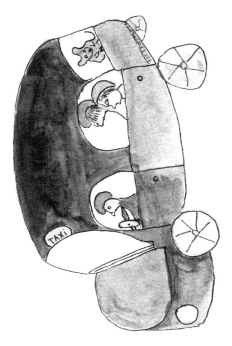

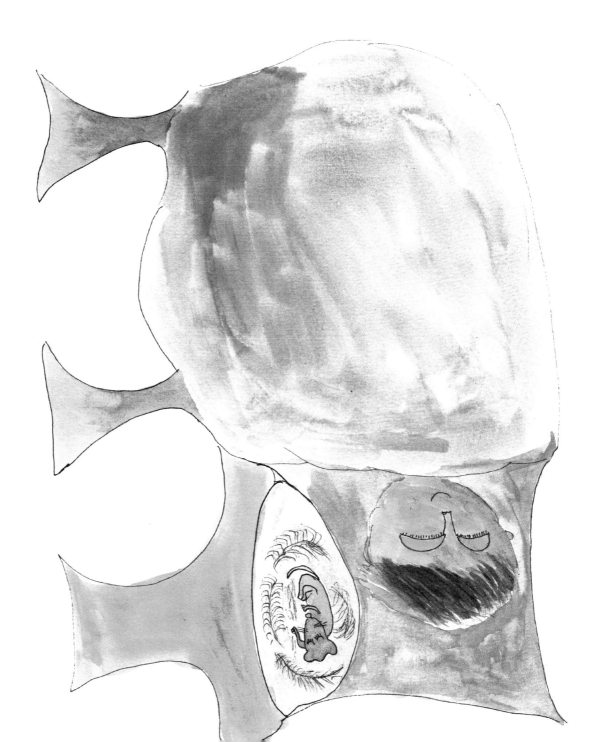

We arrived at our hotel, ate pea soup, and fell fast asleep beneath the blue satin sheets.

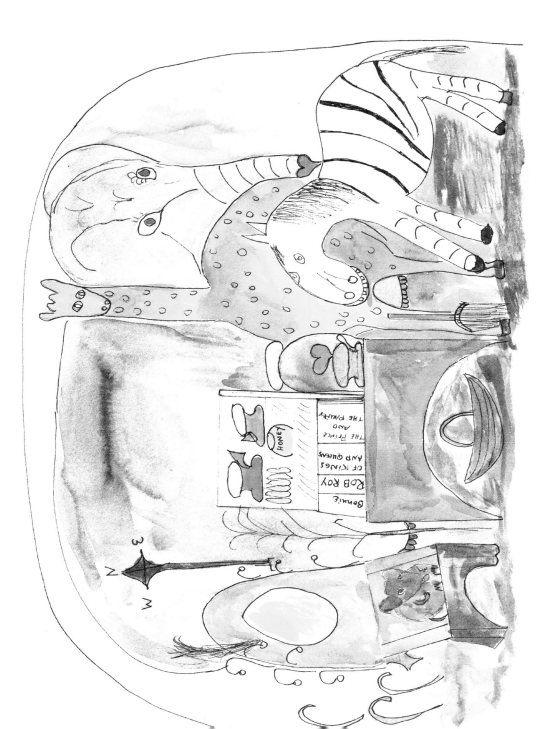

The next day, we went to see Buckingham Palace, St. James Court, the Crown Jewels in the Tower of London, and then to Portobello Road. Shops lined the street and there was even a grinning zebra.

Quite exhausted, we sat down for high tea. Out from my purse jumped Penelope, who exclaimed, "Quite famished I am!"

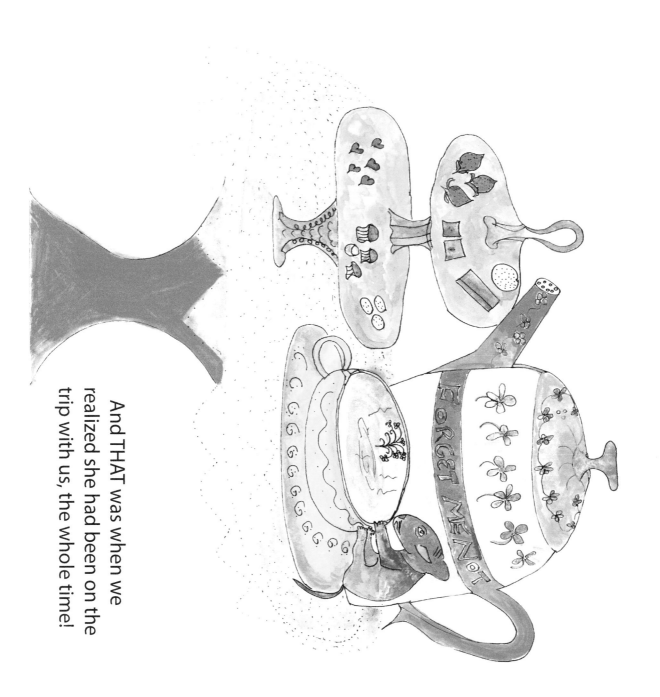

And THAT was when we realized she had been on the trip with us, the whole time!

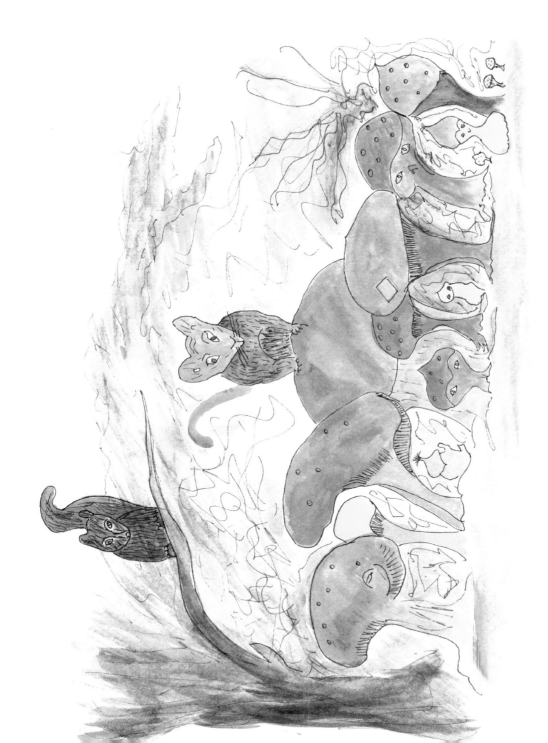

As we explored London, Penelope also went exploring.

Penelope went to Buckingham Palace.

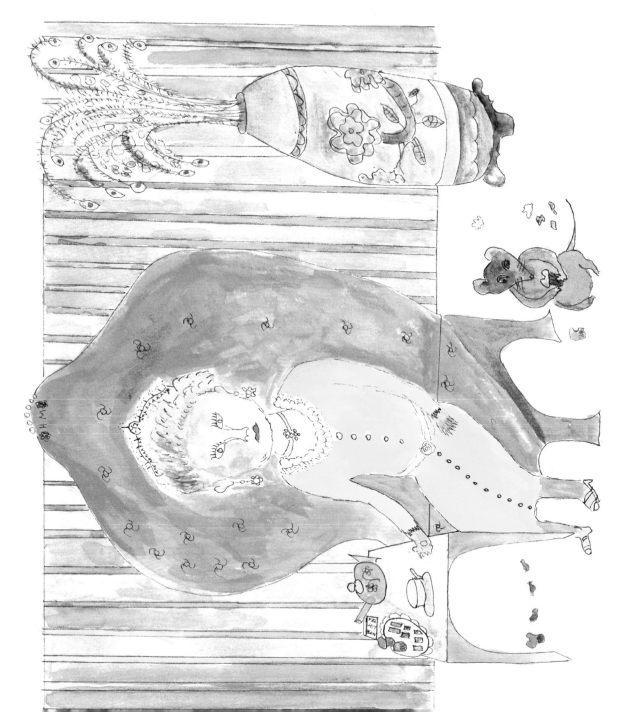

Then Penelope had tea with Her Majesty, the Queen! Penelope preferred the strawberry jam served with Devonshire cream with her crumpets.

Penelope found out many things from Her Majesty. The Queen's grandfather dearly loved her and he gave her special things, like miniature dogs and horses. He put them in a box that the Queen keeps at the foot of her bed. Penelope went room by room until she found Her Majesty's room and then Penelope peeked inside the chest and saw many lovely secrets!

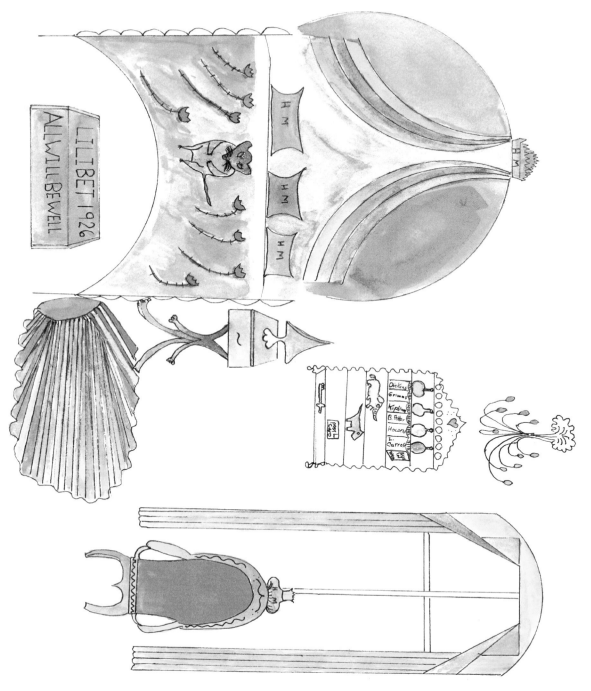

LILIBET 1926
ALL WILL BE WELL

Sadly, our vacation was ending and it was time to fly home. Penelope suddenly blurted out, "We must go to my favorite tea shop one more time!" And off she went and we hurried after her.

Penelope led us to an old Tudor building down by the River Thames. We were all having tea, when Penelope, in her curious way, decided to investigate a little hole-in-the-wall.

Penelope saw a naughty muskrat trying to steal a crumpet.
"You must say, 'May I *please* have a cup of tea and a crumpet?'" she
shouted. So surprised was the muskrat that she ran out the door.
The shopkeeper said, "Oh you saved the day from the sneaky
muskrat, and now you can stay as long as you like!" Penelope
thought for a moment or two.

Penelope finally answered, "I would like to live in Buckingham Palace!"

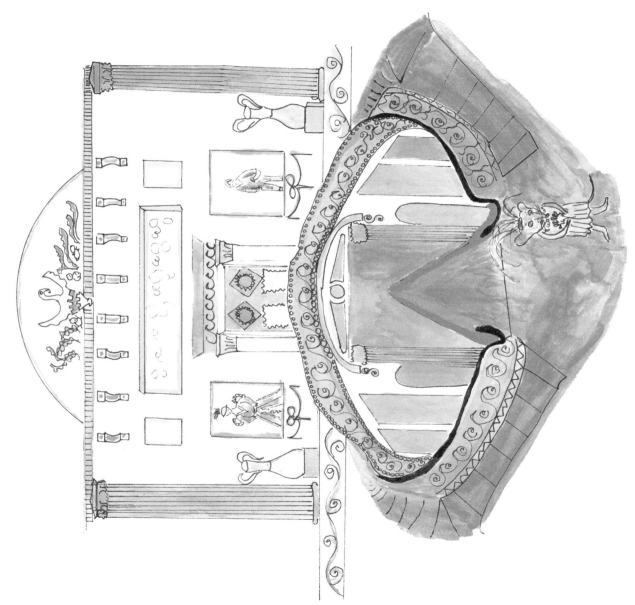

And THAT is what she did! Penelope had many invitations. She went to High Tea, Trooping of the Colour, and on carriage rides. "And I have a posie for Her Majesty!"

After a summer of fun and frolicking around London, Penelope suddenly missed Moi. So she packed up her bag and flew home to us!

FACTS:

HIGH TEA is a British tradition, served from 5pm to 7pm, and it can take the place of dinner. A typical table arrangement includes lovely flowers, china teacups and a silver tea service. The food served at High Tea may include:

- **CRUMPETS** are round little biscuits that one spreads Devonshire cream on.
- **DEVONSHIRE CREAM** is lovely, fluffy cream from cows of Devonshire.
- **SCONES** are biscuits, typically made with raisins and other berries.
- **TEA SANDWICHES** are typically cut in shapes and have the crusts cut off the bread. They are filled with all kinds of edibles and spreads, including watercress or cucumber with cream cheese, cucumber with dill, egg salad, and smoked salmon.
- **MEATS**, like roast beef and sliced ham, are served with different flavors of chutney.
- **CHUTNEY** is an Indian condiment that is prepared in several ways: sweet, sour, hot, citric, smooth, and lumpy with fruits, blended into a variety of flavors. Some common chutneys are mixed with coriander (cilantro), mint, coconut, onion, prune, chili, mango, lime, and garlic.
- **DESSERTS** include bite-size tarts, cakes, or trifle.
- **TRIFLE** is a sponge cake moistened with sherry, egg custard pudding, strawberries, and whipped cream with slivered almonds.
- **THE TEA** that is served can be a variety of teas flavored with mint or ginger, black teas, or teas mixed with fragrant flowers, such as elderberry or jasmine. Now, green teas are served for their antioxidant attributes. Just ask Penelope; she is a connoisseur of tea varieties.

A **POSY** is a small, colorful flower bouquet fastened together in a bunch, which is meant to be held in your hand.

The Union Jack, UK

ROYAL FLAGS Precocious Penelope hoisted her own flag up on the roof of Buckingham Palace. Usually, that space is reserved for the Queen's flag, the ROYAL STANDARD. It is flown on top of the Queen's castles when she is in residence. The Royal Standard flag can also be flown on top of your house if the Queen decides to visit you. If the UNION JACK is flying at Buckingham Palace or Windsor Castle, instead of the Royal Standard, the Queen is not in residence.

The Royal Standard

ROYAL CARRIAGES There are over 100 carriages and coaches that belong to Her Majesty. Most are kept in the Royal Mews next to Buckingham Palace. There are days when the Mews are open to the public. Many of the coaches are used for various events. The glass coach is for royal weddings. Some of the others are used for processions, events, and celebrations, such as Royal Ascot, Kings Troop, Royal Horse Artillery, and Trooping of the Colour.

TROOPING THE COLOUR

TROOPING THE COLOUR is the official Birthday of the British Sovereign. This ceremonial parade is usually held on a Saturday in mid-June. The parade comprises of foot guards, mounted horse guards, King's Troop and Royal Artillery, carrying all the flags of the monarchy. Several marching bands join the pomp and ceremony. They start at the Royal Mews and march along Buckingham Palace, through the gardens and into St. James Park. It is a military tradition that dates back two hundred years. The Queen herself rode horseback during this procession until 1987. Her Majesty, Queen Elizabeth II was born on April 21, 1926.

MUSKRATS

MUSKRATS are very smart, adaptable, social creatures who build reed and stick lodges for their families, along waterways, much like beavers do. They are aquatic mammals that look like rather large mice, with short fur. Their feet are partially webbed which gives these animals quite an advantage when swimming. Like beavers they tend to have great lung capacity and can stay under water for quite a long time; more than ten minutes by some estimates. They mark their territories with a musk smell. Once a North American creature, the muskrat has taken up residency on most continents of the world where river valleys, marshes, ponds, and lush planting habitats have allowed muskrats to flourish.

It appears that the muskrat has developed a special penchant for the area along the Thames River, near London, because their lodges have been found along this river and in nearby marshes. Muskrats have also discovered London to be very welcoming because of all the food scraps that they find along the river and in the street gutters. It is a curious little creature that has probably traveled the world aboard ships. London and the areas around the city have become a wonderful landing zone for the little, versatile muskrat.

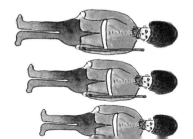

THE GRAND STAIRCASE

THE GRAND STAIRCASE For visitors who receive an invitation to visit Queen Elizabeth at Buckingham Palace, one is ushered into the Grand Hall and up the curving marble stairs of the "Grand Staircase." Then one continues along a hallway to one of the fabulous sun-lit, elegant rooms, for a special High Tea with Her Majesty, Queen Elizabeth! One can only imagine what great fun it was for Penelope, The Tea Mouse, to be invited to join Queen Elizabeth for a special tea time and to also explore Buckingham Palace!

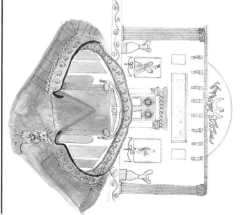

Pastry Illustrations (see previous page) copyright © 2013 Katherine Gladsky
Fact Sources:

Goodwin, Lindsey. "Traditional English Tea Sandwiches." About Food. http://coffeetea.about.com/od/foodmeetsdrinks/tp/Traditional-English-Tea-Sandwiches.htm

Raeside, Rob. "United Kingdom: Use and Status of the Flag." Flags of the World. 2011. http://www.crwflags.com/fotw/flags/gb-use.html.

"Royal Residences: Buckingham Palace." Official Website of the British Royal Family. https://www.royal.uk/royal-residences-buckingham-palace.

"Trooping the Colour." Wikipedia. https://en.wikipedia.org/wiki/Trooping_the_Colour#Notes.

Thank you for spending time with
Penelope and me in our whimsical world.
Stay tuned for more exciting stories from
Holden's Whimsicals.

Coming Soon!

~ Helen W. Holden

Portrait Photography by Laura Almada

CPSIA information can be obtained
at www.ICGtesting.com
Printed in the USA
LVOW06*003617041?

531049LV00012B/31/P

9 780988 726918